Hannah Augsbach Lamma

I dedicate this book to all essential workers and anyone affected by COVID-19. We are *all* in this together.

Josie was a happy girl,
busy as could be.
From theater to karate to school to dance,
her time was never free.

Then her world turned upside down,
she was forced to stay at home.
The Corona virus was a national threat
and kept everyone alone.

At first Josie was excited,
time for family and fun.
But after a couple long weeks being in,
her joy started to run.

She couldn't go to practice
or see any of her friends.
the days started to feel longer,
she wanted this thing to end.

Her parents were stressed working.
The news brought fright and gloom,
and though Josie tried her best,
it was hard to learn over Zoom.

It all became too much one day;
Josie started to cry.
Everything changed around her;
She didn't understand why.

When Josie woke the next morning,
her mom was hard at work.
She was sewing bits of cloth together,
finishing with a smirk.

Her mom saw Josie's confusion,
"They're masks for us to wear.
I'm making them for our family
to stay safe and show we care."

"That way when we go out,
germs can't come or leave.
We are much less likely to get sick,
until there's a cure to receive."

And people, like Aunt Jamie,
who are working the frontline,
need all the help they can get,
and all we have is time."

Josie thought this was fitting;
everything clicked in her head.
She knew that heroes always wore masks
from the comic books she read.

She did think something was missing
from the brand new uniform.
She grabbed some of the leftover cloth
and quickly began to transform.

She wrapped a sheet around her neck
and tied the ends in a bow.
She grabbed a matching patterned piece
to give to her mom to sew.

Her mom loved the idea;
they knew what they had to do.
With all the time and supplies in their hands,
they had to be heroes, too.

So Josie got busy once more,
sewing with her mom.
The days she now spent working,
slowly restored her calm.

These people were always heroes,
now they looked the part.
When she saw their smiling faces,
it warmed Josie's heart.

Josie and her mom drove around,
giving out the masks and capes.
For each and every person
picking new colors, patterns, and shapes.

Masks for the nurses and doctors,
teachers and police too.
For the grocery store workers,
it's the least that they could do.

School may look different,
six feet apart with masks.
But to keep her friends and teachers safe,
these weren't difficult tasks!

Josie should be our example;
we all have to do our part.
Wearing masks and keeping distance
will show you're kind and smart!

So wear your masks and be good today,
it's not that hard to do.
By doing these simple things,
you'll be a hero, too!

Hannah Augsbach Lamma is a high school senior who hopes Josie the Superhero will help children that have trouble expressing their emotions about a pandemic environment feel understood and inspired. She hopes to read this book to her kids one day, show them that you can find positives in any situation, and that difficult times never last forever.

CPSIA information can be obtained
at www.ICGtesting.com
Printed in the USA
LVHW070939241020
669130LV00058B/450